PIXAR
Storybook
Collection

Disney PRESS

LOS ANGELES • NEW YORK

Contents

"Mighty Mom" written by Courtney Carbone. Copyright © 2021 Disney Enterprises, Inc., and Pixar.

"Back on Earth" written by Kelsey Sullivan. Originally published in *5-Minute Disney*Pixar Stories*. Copyright © 2019 Disney Enterprises, Inc., and Pixar.

"Pepita and Dante to the Rescue!" written by Angela Dominguez. Copyright © 2018 Disney Enterprises, Inc., and Pixar.

"Moving Day" written by Kate Egan. Originally published in *Toy Story Storybook Collection*. Copyright © 2010 Disney Enterprises, Inc., and Pixar.

"Night-Lights" written by Josh Crute. Originally published in *Bedtime Favorites Storybook Collection*. Copyright © 2019 Disney Enterprises, Inc., and Pixar.

"Night Games" written by Elizabeth Rudnick. Copyright © 2016 Disney Enterprises, Inc., and Pixar.

"Rally to the Finish!" written by Annie Auerbach. Copyright © 2013 Disney Enterprises, Inc., and Pixar.

"What I Did on My Summer Vacation" written by Annie Auerbach. Copyright © 2012 Disney Enterprises, Inc., and Pixar.

"A Winning Friendship" written by John Edwards. Originally published in *Bedtime Favorites Storybook Collection*. Copyright © 2019 Disney Enterprises, Inc., and Pixar.

"Soul" adapted by Kelsey Sullivan from the book *Soul Read-Along Storybook & CD*, written by Bill Scollon. Copyright © 2020 Disney Enterprises, Inc., and Pixar.

"A Day Out with Mom" written by Suzanne Francis. Originally published in *5-Minute Girl Power Stories*. Copyright © 2018 Disney Enterprises, Inc., and Pixar.

"The Big Campout" adapted from the story "Starry Night," written by Wendy Loggia. Copyright © 2011 Disney Enterprises, Inc., and Pixar.

"The Riley and Bing Bong Band" written by Suzanne Francis. Copyright © 2016 Disney Enterprises, Inc., and Pixar.

"You're It, Dory!" written by Bonita Garr. Originally published in *5-Minute Under the Sea Stories*. Copyright © 2016 Disney Enterprises, Inc., and Pixar.

"A Delicious Duo" written by Lauren Clauss. Originally published in *5-Minute Disney*Pixar Stories*. Copyright © 2019 Disney Enterprises, Inc., and Pixar.

"A New Purpose" adapted by Megan Roth from the book *Toy Story 4 Read-Along Storybook & CD*, written by Bill Scollon. Copyright © 2019 Disney Enterprises, Inc., and Pixar.

"Arlo's Birthday Adventure" written by Brooke Vitale. Originally published in *5-Minute Disney*Pixar Stories*. Copyright © 2019 Disney Enterprises, Inc., and Pixar.

"A Gift for Giulia" written by Josh Crute. Copyright © 2021 Disney Enterprises, Inc., and Pixar.

All illustrations by the Disney Storybook Art Team

Published by Disney Press, an imprint of Buena Vista Books, Inc. No part of this book may be reproduced or transmitted in any form or by any means, electronic or mechanical, including photocopying, recording, or by any information storage and retrieval system, without written permission from the publisher.

For information address Disney Press, 1200 Grand Central Avenue, Glendale, California 91201.

Printed in the United States of America

First Hardcover Edition, April 2022

Library of Congress Control Number: 2021946418

10 9 8 7 6 5 4 3 2 1

ISBN 978-1-368-06662-4

FAC-034274-22049

For more Disney Press fun, visit www.disneybooks.com

Mighty Mom

Early one morning, Ian, Barley, and Laurel Lightfoot arrived at Manticore's Tavern. The Manticore directed the construction crew as they tore away the tavern's modern façade. Soon it would be returned to its former glory as a quest landmark.

"Thank goodness you're here!" exclaimed the Manticore. "The reopening is coming up fast, and I need all the help I can get."

The Lightfoots didn't waste any time. Ian used magic to summon equipment from the supply closet. Laurel grabbed a sledgehammer and began to tear down a wall. A few spiders crawled out of the hole she'd made.

"Ugh!" Laurel cried. "I hate spiders."

Ian laughed. "Mom, you fought a dragon. Spiders are nothing!"

"They're so creepy! I'd rather fight a dragon," Laurel said. She continued to knock down the wall.

As Laurel worked, she came across an old nameplate.

"'Chantar's Talon,'" she read. "Where does it go?"

"Nowhere. I never actually found the talon!" The Manticore laughed. "I had always planned to go on a quest to retrieve it, but I got too busy running the tavern."

"According to legend," Ian said, pulling the *Quests of Yore* book from his backpack, "Chantar's Talon brought endless prosperity."

"We'll find it and display it at the grand reopening!" Laurel said.

"I love that idea!" exclaimed the Manticore. "The map burned up in the fire, but the Whispering Elm knows the way."

As the group prepared to leave, Laurel realized something. "How dangerous will this be?"

"Oh, it'll be easy for you three," said the Manticore.

The Lightfoots arrived at a grocery store called Journey Mart. A Whispering Elm was handing out flyers by the front door.

"Hello," said Laurel. "Can you tell us how to find Chantar's Talon?"

"Wow! That really takes me back," said the Elm. "You must reach the center of the labyrinth and face the mighty Minotaur!"

The Lightfoots looked at one another nervously.

"My friend Willow will help," said the Elm, pointing to another tree in the distance.

Willow sent the family to the top of a hill. They were confused by what they saw on the other side.

"Chantar's Talon is in . . . the mall?" said Ian.

"Of course!" exclaimed Barley. "The Labyrinth Mall was once an actual labyrinth."

Inside the mall, the Lightfoots studied a giant map.

Laurel flagged down a security guard. "Excuse me? Could you tell us how to get to the center of the mall?"

"Make a right and then a left and another right," the Minotaur said dully.

The Lightfoots followed the guard's instructions. But all they found was a children's play area.

Laurel pointed to the giant ball pit. "There's a Minotaur in the center!"

The family jumped into the ball pit. A golden crest on the Minotaur's pedestal caught Ian's eye. Laurel pulled the padding away from the pedestal and found a blocked archway.

"The Animate Spell should do the trick," said Ian. *"Presto Avar!"*

The bricks moved!

After the Lightfoots entered, the bricks slammed back into place. They were plunged into total darkness.

"Flame Infernar!" Ian shouted. A bright flame ignited at the top of his staff, illuminating an ancient stone staircase.

Barley created a torch and led the way.

"Looks like the only way out is forward."

The group made
their way to a
massive chamber.
They shuffled along
together. Barley
moved to the back
with his torch, and
Laurel kept looking
around. She was
anticipating the worst.

"Something doesn't
feel right to me," Laurel said,
coming to a halt. "Why haven't we run into anyone . . . or anything?"

She found a discarded suit of armor on the ground and put it on. "Maybe
this will come in handy!"

"I'll see if the Danger Detection Spell can help us," said Ian.

The top of the staff glowed an ominous deep red.

Suddenly, a giant spider scooped up all three of them and wove them tighter and tighter into its web. Ian's staff clattered to the floor, out of reach.

"The Manticore said this quest would be easy!" cried Ian.

"Why did it have to be a spider?" added Laurel.

Just when all hope seemed to be lost, Barley spotted something in an alcove below them.

"Chantar's Talon!" he exclaimed. "It's right there!"

They could finish this quest after all!

Barley reached and reached, but it was no use. They were too far away. Then Laurel had an idea.

Laurel used a sharp edge of the armor to cut them down. Although she managed to escape, the boys were still trapped in the web! She dashed toward an ax across the chamber.

Laurel faced the creature. "If I can defeat a dragon, I can defeat you!" She dodged, weaved, and rolled so quickly that the spider became disoriented.

With the spider confused, Laurel freed the boys from the web.

"Way to go, Mom!" cheered Barley.

Ian grabbed his staff. They needed a diversion to escape.

"Cumulo Mystara!" Ian cried.

The room filled with thick fog. As the spider struggled to see, Laurel sprinted to the alcove and grabbed the talon.

"Got it!" she shouted. "Now let's get out of here!"

The Lightfoots ran out of the chamber just as the last of the fog cleared.

The family managed to find their way out of the tunnel and the mall.
They arrived back at the tavern.

"You did it!" the Manticore exclaimed. She placed the talon on the wall
with her other relics. "I'm finally ready for the grand reopening!"

"I gotta hand it to you, Mom," Barley said. "That was pretty cool."

"We're lucky to have such a fearless and mighty mom!" Ian added.

Laurel smiled and gave them a big hug.

"Let's plan our next adventure!" she said.

Back on Earth

After the *Axiom* **landed** back on Earth, the Captain wanted to help all the passengers and robots aboard the ship adjust to the changes life on the planet would bring.

He knew that by working together, they could all make Earth their home . . . even after having lived only on a luxury spaceship in outer space. WALL·E and EVE wanted to help the Captain.

WALL•E was happy to be back on Earth and even happier not to be lonely anymore. He watched his favorite movies with EVE, collected even more new treasures with his robot friends, and still tidied up the planet— one piece of trash at a time.

EVE was
having a harder
time finding
something to
do on Earth. Her
original directive
was to scan the planet for
any sign of plant life . . . and she'd found it.

Now she wasn't sure how to

fill her days. So she

just flew around,

still scanning

and

scanning

and

scanning.

One day the Captain noticed EVE wandering around aimlessly. He had to help her somehow. The Captain went to WALL•E, hoping that together they'd find a new purpose perfectly suited for EVE.

"I want everyone to feel at home here. But EVE seems like she's looking for something. Can you help me?" he asked.

WALL·E beeped in agreement. He quickly rolled home to think of a plan to cheer up EVE.

After a few days of thinking it over, WALL·E had the perfect idea: he would give EVE her very own one-of-a-kind garden!

EVE already knew how to find plant life, but maybe now she could make plant life grow. And even better, all their robot friends could help. He knew EVE would love her garden even more if it was something they created together.

WALL•E thought his friends could first help by clearing the land around his house. They removed rocks, roots, sticks, and trash from the soil, making sure it was perfect for whatever EVE wanted to grow.

Then WALL•E built a fence around the piece of land using his compacted-trash units.

Next his friends helped him gather some supplies. EVE would need seeds, plant bulbs, and gardening tools.

When the time finally came to show EVE what they had made, WALL•E could barely contain his excitement.

They arrived, and WALL•E told EVE that this garden was hers to take care of. She stared in amazement and then got to work!

She even assigned some jobs to her friends.

EVE thought VAQ-M would be perfect at planting seeds. Moments later, VAQ-M was sneezing seeds into holes WALL•E had made.

In the corner, EVE was planting some flowers and vegetables that needed less sun than the rest of the garden. She knew exactly who could help!

BRL-A could open his canopy and guard the plants from the sun as they started to grow.

EVE thought M O would
be able to help her
clean the fruits
and vegetables.

He was
delighted
to help. "Foreign
contaminants!" M-O cheered.

Then EVE walked VN-GO to the fence WALL•E had built. VN-GO
was ecstatic to find a blank canvas to showcase his art. Even if the paint
splashed everywhere, it still made the boxes of trash look more beautiful!

A few days later, the Captain visited WALL•E and EVE's home to check on their progress. He was thrilled to see WALL•E's plan had worked. Managing a garden really was the perfect job for EVE! She looked happier than he'd seen her since they had returned to Earth.

But then he noticed EVE flying back and forth—and then back and forth again—with a watering can.

Hmmm . . . he thought.

"EVE!" the
Captain called.
"I have an
idea for your
garden.
What if you
built a well? I bet
you could just
burrow down
here. It gets
water here faster, and
you wouldn't have to
fly back and forth so
much filling your watering
can. Then you could concentrate on the planting. What do you think?"

EVE beeped excitedly. She *loved* the idea!

For the first time back on Earth, EVE felt like she had a new directive. Over time, her garden grew. It wasn't long before EVE and WALL•E had gardens surrounding their home.

"WALL•E !" EVE said happily. Her gardens became her favorite places on Earth. She loved spending time surrounded by her plants, with her favorite robot by her side.

Pepita and Dante
to the Rescue!

In the little Mexican town of Santa Cecilia, the Rivera family was busy preparing for a big celebration called Día de los Muertos—the Day of the Dead. They were honoring and remembering their ancestors by making an altar called an ofrenda. It held photographs, keepsakes, and food—everything that the Rivera ancestors had loved in life. The family hung beautiful paper banners called papel picado around the room and arranged a path of marigold petals that would lead the spirits of their loved ones back home.

For nearly a year, Miguel had been filling the house with music. It was easy for him now that he had his family's approval. The music brought them all closer together.

Miguel finished singing for his mamá and his little sister, Socorro.

"Bravo, Miguel!" said Mamá. "Now, can my little músico see if Abuelita needs help in the kitchen?"

Miguel's stomach rumbled. "Sure, Mamá!" he said.

As Miguel approached the kitchen, he noticed Dante and Pepita near the door. Abuelita enjoyed having Dante around more than she once had, but she had a strict no-animal policy in the kitchen.

"Come back a little later," Miguel whispered. "Abuelita will give us tamales."

Dante wagged his tail and Pepita meowed as they left.

The kitchen was filled with the smells of scrumptious food.

"Do you need help, Abuelita?" asked Miguel.

"I'm okay, mi hijo, but eat something," Abuelita said as she continued stirring. Abuelita was making the family's favorite dishes: posole, pan de muerto, mole rojo, and much more. The food would be placed on the ofrenda as an offering for their loved ones who were no longer there.

Miguel realized something. "Abuelita, what are you making for Papá Héctor?"

Abuelita dropped her wooden spoon with a loud clatter.

"¡Ay, Dios mío! I don't know! I didn't even know who he was until last year!"

Suddenly, Miguel realized he needed Dante and Pepita. "I have an idea, Abuelita. Uh . . . I'll be right back."

Miguel rushed off to find Dante and Pepita. They were the only ones who could help him. His family had no idea that Dante and Pepita had a secret! They were creatures of the spirit realm who could travel between the Lands of the Living and the Dead. Miguel ran down the streets of Santa Cecilia.

He found Dante and Pepita taking a nap in the gazebo near Mariachi Plaza. "I need both of you. Can you help me?" Miguel asked.

Dante barked, and Pepita purred. Miguel exhaled. "Thanks! Can you get Papá Héctor a message?" He handed Dante a note.

Dante wagged his tail before dashing away with Pepita.

Dante and Pepita dodged around crowds in the cemetery and ran all
the way to the Marigold Bridge, which could be seen only by visiting
spirits. As soon as they reached the bridge, they magically glowed as they
transformed. Pepita grew from a little alley cat into a mighty flying jaguar,
while Dante sprouted a pair of wings.

"*Rooooo-roo-roo-roo,*" mumbled Dante, trying not to drop Miguel's note.

He spotted a few of the dead Riveras near Marigold Grand Central Station.

The dead Riveras looked up and saw the two spirit guides overhead.

"Look, it's Pepita!" shouted Tío Felipe.

"And Dante!" said Tía Victoria.

When Dante and Pepita landed, they gave the note to Mamá Coco, who now lived in the Land of the Dead. "It's urgent," she said, reading the note. "Miguel needs to know what my papá wants for the ofrenda."

"Follow us to the plaza!" said Tía Victoria.

The plaza was filled with a giant crowd. Mamá Imelda noticed the spirit guides and stopped singing. "¿Qué pasa? Why are Dante and Pepita here?"

Mamá Coco handed the note to Papá Héctor. He was touched that Miguel was concerned about his first Día de los Muertos. After he wrote down his favorite dishes, he gave the note back to Dante.

The dead Riveras waved goodbye as Dante and Pepita soared into the sky. Pepita swooped toward the Land of the Living. Dante veered slightly off course, greeting other spirit creatures nearby. But Pepita knew they were running out of time. She grabbed Dante with her talons and placed him on her back for safekeeping.

"Rooooo-roo-roo-roo!" Dante crooned as they flew over the Marigold Bridge.

Dante and Pepita transformed back into a dog and cat when they returned to Santa Cecilia. They dashed toward the Rivera house.

Miguel gave them a big hug when they arrived. "Thank you, Dante and Pepita! You two saved the day!"

Miguel could not reveal Dante's and Pepita's secret identities. Instead, he told Abuelita that he found the list in one of Mamá Coco's journals. She took the list from Miguel and kissed his head. "¡Gracias, Miguelito! I have just enough time to make these dishes before the festivities begin."

Later that night, Papá Héctor, Mamá Imelda, Mamá Coco, and the rest of the Rivera ancestors crossed over the Marigold Bridge.

They walked through the cemetery and followed the path of marigolds that their family had left for them.

When the dead Riveras arrived at the house, they admired the ofrenda that the family had worked so hard to put together.

The whole Rivera family, both the living and the dead, enjoyed the celebration together. Even Dante and Pepita joined in on the festivities. Miguel strummed his guitar as Dante and Pepita enjoyed their well-deserved tamales.

Moving Day

id was Andy's next-door neighbor. He wasn't very nice to his toys. He'd take them apart, then attach one toy's head or legs to another's body.

Sid had won Woody the cowboy and Buzz Lightyear the space ranger in a game at Pizza Planet. Woody and Buzz had been at the restaurant looking for Andy.

As Woody looked around Sid's room, some of Sid's toys came out from their hiding places.

"They're gonna eat us, Buzz!" Woody yelled. "Use your karate-chop action."

Woody and Buzz managed to escape from Sid's toys. They ran out into the hallway and came face to face with Sid's dog, Scud. Woody ducked into a closet. Buzz hid in a dark room behind the door.

Suddenly, Buzz heard someone saying, "Calling Buzz Lightyear. This is Star Command."

Buzz looked up at the TV. The voice was coming from an ad for Buzz Lightyear toys. It continued, "The world's greatest superhero—now the world's greatest toy."

NOT A FLYING TOY

Buzz stared in shock at the TV. He couldn't believe what he had just heard. He wondered if Woody had been right all along. Was he really just a toy?

The space ranger walked out of the room feeling sad. He looked out an open window at the blue sky and watched a bird fly by. He kept hearing Woody's voice in his head saying, *"You are a toy! You can't fly!"*

He hung his head against the railing over the stairs. Then he had an idea. He would prove to Woody that he could fly. He *was* a space ranger!

Buzz climbed up and stood on top of the railing. He opened his wings. Then he leapt.

"To infinity and beyond!" he called out.

He hung in the air for a moment and then started to fall. He crashed on the floor at the bottom of the stairs, breaking off his left arm.

When Woody found him, Buzz was upset, but he understood that he was a toy.

Woody was desperate to get them both back to Andy's house. He ran to the open window and called out, "Hey, guys!"

Andy's toys appeared in the window next door. They were surprised Woody was there.

"Oh, boy, am I glad to see you guys," Woody said. "Here, catch this." He tossed a string of Christmas lights over to them so he and Buzz could climb across.

But Buzz wouldn't move. Woody held out Buzz's broken arm to show that he was with him.

The other toys didn't believe Woody. They thought he had hurt their new friend.

Woody felt terrible. When he turned around to tell Buzz, he saw Sid's mutant toys closing in around the space ranger. Woody ran over to hold them back, but they took Buzz's arm and pushed the cowboy away.

Then, after a few minutes, the mutant toys stepped away from Buzz. They'd reattached his arm! Woody couldn't believe it.

Suddenly, the other toys scurried off. Sid was coming! Woody hid under a milk crate, but Buzz wouldn't move.

When Sid walked in the room, he held out a rocket. "I've always wanted to put a spaceman into orbit," he said. Then he taped the rocket to Buzz.

Sid was about to take Buzz outside when he saw a flash of lightning. "Oh, no!" Sid cried. He looked at the rocket. The launch would just have to wait until tomorrow.

All night, Woody tried to convince Buzz to help him escape. He knew Andy's family was moving the next day and they had to get home.

But Buzz didn't care about going home. "Andy's house, Sid's house, what's the difference?" he said. "I'm just a little, insignificant toy."

"Look," Woody said, "over in that house is a kid who thinks you are the greatest. And it's not because you're a space ranger, pal. It's because you're a toy! You're *his* toy."

Woody tried to convince Buzz all night long. But Buzz didn't even move until he looked at the bottom of his boot. Andy had written his name there. Then Buzz knew what he had to do.

He walked over to Woody. "Come on, Sheriff," he said. "There's a kid over in that house who needs us."

Buzz helped Woody out from under the milk crate. But before they could escape, Sid woke up and grabbed Buzz. "Time for liftoff!" he cried as he ran out of the room.

Woody asked Sid's toys to help him. "We're going to have to break a few rules," he said. "But if it works, it'll help everybody." The toys came up with a plan and raced outside. Buzz was in position to be launched.

Sid got ready to light the rocket. Suddenly, he heard a voice. He looked around and saw Woody. He picked up the cowboy.

Then Sid's toys came out from their hiding places in the yard. Soon Sid was surrounded by all the toys he'd hurt.

Sid looked at the toys around him. As each one came closer, he panicked more and more.

Woody kept speaking to Sid, which made the boy even more scared. "From now on, you must take good care of your toys. Because if you don't, we'll find out, Sid." Then Woody leaned in close and pointed at Sid. "So play nice!"

Sid screamed and dropped Woody. He ran into the house and slammed the door. The toys cheered!

Woody helped Buzz down off the launching pad. That's when he saw the moving truck pulling out of Andy's driveway.

Woody ran through the hole in the fence. But the rocket on Buzz's back got stuck. "Just go," Buzz called to Woody. "I'll catch up."

When Woody realized Buzz was stuck, he ran back to help him. The two toys ran down the street chasing the truck. Buzz was the first one there. He grabbed a loose strap and pulled himself up on the truck's bumper. Woody was right behind him.

"Come on," Buzz said. "You can do it, Woody!"

Woody grabbed the strap and started to pull himself up. But something grabbed his boot. It was Scud!

Buzz saved Woody by jumping onto Scud's head. But the truck was moving away quickly.

Woody climbed into the back of the van and rummaged through the boxes. The other toys didn't know what he was doing.

Finally, Woody found what he was looking for—RC Car! He sent RC out after Buzz. But Andy's other toys were upset with Woody. They still thought he'd hurt Buzz, so they pushed him out of the truck.

Then they watched as Buzz and RC picked up Woody. Buzz had the remote control and was speeding toward the truck. The toys realized that it had all been a misunderstanding.

Slinky Dog stretched himself out as far as he could, but they still couldn't get close enough. Suddenly, RC started slowing down. His batteries had run out.

Woody watched sadly as the truck drove away. Then Buzz remembered the rocket on his back. They lit it and zoomed closer to the truck. RC landed easily in the back. But Woody and Buzz were launched into the sky.

Buzz snapped open his wings, and he and Woody broke free of the rocket.

"Buzz, you're flying!" Woody exclaimed.

"This isn't flying," Buzz said. "This is falling with style."

The two toys flew toward Andy's car. They dropped through the open sunroof and landed safely on the back seat.

Andy turned and saw the cowboy and space ranger. "Woody! Buzz!" he shouted. He was happy to have his two favorite toys back.

Woody and Buzz settled into Andy's new house with the rest of his toys. They were happy to be home.

When Christmas rolled around, the toys sat near the baby monitor to listen as Andy opened his gifts.

"You're not worried, are you?" Woody asked Buzz.

"No," Buzz replied nervously. "Are you?"

"Now, Buzz, what could Andy possibly get that is worse than you?" Woody teased.

They listened as the first present was opened. *Woof! Woof!*

"Wow! A puppy!" Andy cried.

Buzz and Woody looked at each other and laughed. At least it wasn't a toy!

Night-Lights

"**I see one! I** see one! Pull over, Mr. Fredricksen!" Russell said. Carl swerved the station wagon to the side of the road.

"Is it a squirrel?" asked Dug as he jumped out of the car.

"Even better!" said Russell. "According to the *Wilderness Explorer Guide to Flora and Fauna*, it's a Japanese morning glory."

They were headed to Sylvan State Park to earn Russell's Better Botanist Badge—his first as a Senior Wilderness Explorer. All he had to do was find and identify ten varieties of wildflower.

"Only nine more to go," he said as he took a photo of the flower.

"We'd better get moving then," Carl said.

As they drove, Russell looked at the flowers in his field guide.

"Wow, this book has everything in it," he said. "It has sunflowers. It has butterfly milkweed. It has purple wisteria."

"Does it have a ghost crocus?" asked Carl with a sly smile.

"A what?" asked Russell.

"A ghost crocus," said Carl. "It's a legendary flower that blooms only at night. Pale as the moon—glows in the dark—with six silver petals and stars on its stamens.

"Brave explorers have looked for it for centuries. Most people don't think it exists, but Ellie swore she saw one once— at the very park we're going to."

"Wow!" said Russell. Then he frowned. "I don't see it in the field guide."

"Like I said, most people don't think it exists," said Carl.

When they reached the park, it was already midmorning.

It took a while to find

their campsite . . .

. . . and set up their tents. By the time they were ready to hike, it was midday.

They spent the day searching for flowers in Russell's guide. By the time the sun was setting, they had found ten varieties of wildflower! But Russell couldn't stop thinking about the ghost crocus.

"Please, Mr. Fredricksen," said Russell as they walked back to the campsite, "can we look for a ghost crocus?"

"Sorry," said Carl. "It's getting late. We have to get back to camp before dark."

That night, they sang beside the campfire and told each other ghost stories.

And then they looked at the constellations.

"All right, it's getting very late. It's time for bed," Carl said, opening his

tent. He had forgotten all about the ghost crocus.

But Russell hadn't. He couldn't sleep knowing there was another flower he could find and identify. Hiking at night might be dangerous for a *Junior* Wilderness Explorer, but Russell was a *Senior* Wilderness Explorer. He knew he could handle it!

"Let's go, Dug," he whispered. "We're gonna go fetch something."

"I *love* fetching," said Dug.

The woods were a lot darker than Russell had expected. Maybe Mr. Fredricksen was right. It was getting very late.

But then he spotted a soft glow. It seemed to be coming from the back of a cave. What he didn't see was the steep drop! Too late! He tumbled down into the mouth of the cave.

"Oh, no! Are you okay?" said Dug. Dug didn't hear a response from the cave, so he ran back to the campsite.

Carl awoke to a wet tongue licking his face.

"It is time to get up! We were out in the dark looking for the ghost flower, and then the small mailman fell into the cave!"

"What?" cried Carl. "Quick! Lead me to him!"

Down in the cave, everything went dark. At first, Russell felt alone and afraid.

But then he remembered: he was a Senior Wilderness Explorer. "I can handle this!" he said to himself. He stood up and saw a glimmer of light. It was coming from around the corner.

"Russell!" someone cried. It was Carl. He had tied a rope to a tree and was lowering himself down into the cave.

"Look!" cried Dug happily. "I have found help!"

"I'm sorry, Russell," said Carl. "I shouldn't have told you that story about the ghost crocus. Honestly, I never believed it myself. Ellie always had a great imagination."

"Well, I found something anyway," said Russell with a sly smile.

"Well, I'll be," said Carl.

The next morning, Russell, Dug, and Carl packed up their things and headed back home.

"The Wilderness Explorers are going to be so excited I found all the wildflowers plus one!" Russell chattered away in the back seat.

"Thank you, Ellie," Carl whispered with a smile.

Night Games

Nemo was enjoying the perfect afternoon. He was playing tag with his octopus friend Pearl. The two friends chased each other from sponge bed to sponge bed.

"Tag, you're it!" Pearl giggled as she tapped Nemo on the back with one of her eight tiny tentacles. "Bet you can't catch me!"

"We'll see about that!" Nemo said as Pearl jetted away, kicking up a large cloud of sand.

Nemo flipped his fins faster and chased Pearl past the edge of the sponge beds. He was just about to tag her when he spotted something tall and wide up ahead.

"What *is* that?" he shouted, pointing a fin over Pearl's head.

"What's *what*?" Pearl asked.

"Come on," Nemo said. "Let's go check it out!"

Nemo swam toward the looming object. It seemed to wave at them in the gentle current.

"W-wait for me!" Pearl called out.

Getting closer, Nemo yelped with excitement. It was a huge seaweed bed! The bed was a giant maze of green and red seaweed. Some spots were almost too dense to swim through, while others formed small pockets of open space. Pearl and Nemo had never seen it before!

"This looks like the perfect hide and seek spot!" Nemo said to Pearl. "Want to play?"

Pearl looked around nervously. The sea had started to turn dark. "I would love to, Nemo, but I think we should head home. It's getting late, and both our dads will be wondering where we are."

Nemo realized Pearl was right. It was time to go home for the night.

When Nemo got back to his sea anemone, his father was waiting. They had dinner, and Nemo told him all about his afternoon playing with Pearl and finding the seaweed bed.

"That sounds like a neat place," Marlin told his son. "But now it's time for bed."

"Aww, come on, Dad," Nemo protested. "Can't I just stay up a little bit longer?"

Marlin shook his head. "Try to get some sleep, Son."

Nemo settled into bed and closed his eyes. He told himself a long bedtime story. He thought about boring things, like math class. He even counted dolphins. But he still wasn't sleepy.

Finally, Nemo got up and swam to his father. "Dad, I can't fall asleep. I've tried, but I just can't. So I was thinking . . ."

Marlin looked up at his son. "Thinking, you say," he replied, trying not to smile. He had a pretty good idea what Nemo had been thinking. "What exactly were you thinking, Son?" he asked anyway.

"I think you and I should go to the seaweed bed now. That way you'll know it's safe and I can go there tomorrow and play with my friends. I promise, when we get back, I'll go right to bed. Please?" Nemo begged.

Marlin looked at his son's hopeful face. Seeing the seaweed bed for himself *did* seem like a good idea. "All right," he said finally. "Let's go take a look at this new find of yours."

"Yes!" Nemo shouted, flipping over in excitement. "Let's go!"

As Marlin and Nemo swam through the reef, Nemo realized he was glad to have his father with him. Everything seemed scarier in the dark.

Squinting, Nemo looked for the seaweed bed. But in the dark, it was nearly impossible to see anything.

"Son," Marlin began, "are you sure the bed is out this far?"

Nemo nodded. "It is! I know it is! I just wish we could see a little bit better!"

Nemo was just about to give up when he saw a light in the distance. The speck drew closer and closer, growing brighter and brighter, until it lit up the water all around Nemo and Marlin. In the middle of the light was the strangest fish Nemo had ever seen.

The new fish had giant lights under her eyes.

"Hi. I'm . . . I'm Nemo," Nemo stammered, amazed.

"Hi!" the other fish said in a friendly singsong. "I'm Lumen."

"It's nice to meet you, Lumen," Marlin said. "I'm Nemo's dad. How come we've never seen you before?"

Lumen fluttered around, causing her light to waver and flicker. "My family and I are nocturnal," she said. "We swim and play at night while everyone else is sleeping."

"Dad and I are being nightturnal, too!" Nemo said. "We're looking for this big seaweed bed I found this afternoon. Do you know where it is?"

"You bet I do!" Lumen said. "That's where I live. Follow me!"

Lumen led Nemo and Marlin to the seaweed bed. "Do you want to play a game?" she asked.

"Yeah!" Nemo shouted. "Can we, Dad? Please?"

Marlin nodded. "Just stay out here in the open," he said. "I'm going to go have a look around."

While the kids played, Marlin explored the seaweed bed to make sure it was safe. Behind him, he could hear his son counting down from one hundred.

"Don't peek!" Marlin heard Lumen shout as she swam off to find a good hiding place.

Marlin pushed through the maze of thick green and red strands, swimming farther and farther into the seaweed bed. Suddenly, he realized how dark and quiet it had become. He could no longer hear Nemo or see Lumen's light!

Marlin spun around. He had no idea where he was! All he could see was seaweed. He was lost!

"Nemo!" he shouted. "Nemo! Where are you?"

But there was no answer.

Flipping his fins, Marlin tried to find his way out.

Just when he was beginning to think he would be stuck in the seaweed bed forever, Marlin spotted a faint light in the distance. "Nemo!" he called, swimming toward it. "Is that you?"

Following the light, Marlin made his way through the seaweed. The strands grew farther apart until finally he hit the open water. There, right where he'd left them, were Nemo and Lumen.

Marlin sighed in relief.

"Dad!" Nemo said excitedly. "There you are! We didn't know where you'd gone! Don't you know better than to go swimming off by yourself in the dark?"

Marlin smiled. "I guess I should have followed my own advice!"

Nemo gave Marlin a hug. "I'm just glad we found you, Dad."

Together, the two said good night to Lumen. As they swam home, Marlin let out a big yawn.

Nemo looked at his father. "When we get home, I think you should go right to bed, Dad," Nemo said with a teasing look in his eye. "You've had more than enough adventure for one day."

Rally to the Finish!

German superstar racer Max Schnell had invited Lightning McQueen and some of the other World Grand Prix racers to the first-ever Black Forest Rally Race Invitational.

Lightning was thrilled! He happily accepted the invitation and asked

Mater, Luigi, and Guido to go along with him as his race crew.

When Team Lightning arrived in Germany, they were greeted at the airport by Max. *"Willkommen!"* he said.

Mater had changed into Materhosen on the plane and couldn't wait to show them off. "I can give you the name of my tailor if you like," he said.

Team Lightning was soon whisked off to a prerace party. At the end of the evening, Lightning told Mater he wanted to head to the Black Forest to practice on the racetrack.

An old gentlecar overheard their plans. "Black Forest at night, eh? Just beware of that *Waldgeister* monster. It's the fastest, scariest monster in the forest."

"A m-m-monster?" said Mater. The old car chuckled and drove off.

"I'm sure that 'monster' is just an old legend," said Lightning as he and Mater drove to the forest.

"I hope yer right," said Mater, relaxing a little. Then he looked at all the surrounding trees. "This place sure is pretty!"

"Especially at top speed!" said Lightning as he revved his engine and took off.

110

"Whee-hoo! This is fun!" yelled Mater. "Last one out of the forest is a rusty tow hitch!"

Following the racetrack, the two best buddies drifted down the fire road, crossed over streams, and cruised across bridges until . . .

. . . they got lost. Lightning had accidentally gone in one direction, and Mater had driven off in another.

"Lightning? Lightning? Hellooooo?" yelled Mater. All Mater heard was the wind howling and the trees creaking.

Suddenly, he felt something brush against him.

"Who's there?" he gasped as he spun around.

A large shadowy figure loomed over him. "The Baldmeister monster! *AHHHHHH!*" Mater screamed as he took off backward. "He's gonna get me!"

Meanwhile, Lightning was driving through a different part of the forest. He heard the screaming and headed toward Mater. "Mater! I'm coming!" he yelled.

Once the two friends were reunited, they found the racetrack and followed it out of the forest.

"The Baldtire monster is real," Mater said, shivering.

Lightning sighed. "Mater, you're just imagining things. That monster is not real."

"He *is* real!" Mater insisted. "I ain't never going back in that forest again!"

Then they raced home together.

The next day was race day! Just before the race began, Mater yelled out to the racers, "You aren't still gonna race in the Black Forest, are you?"

"Why wouldn't we?" asked one of the cars.

"Because there's a monster that lives in there!" exclaimed Mater.

The green flag dropped—and the cars were off!

All of a sudden, the racers heard a low grumbling that shook the forest floor.

Then Lightning felt something brush his side and heard a creaking sound.

The racers stopped in their tracks and looked at each other, panic-stricken.

"Maybe Mater was right," said Lightning.

All the racers took off! They sped down a rocky slope and skidded around turns. They saw shadows quickly creeping up behind them.

A ravine was just ahead of them. The racers didn't think twice. They raced forward at full speed and leapt over it!

Lightning and the other cars raced for their lives toward the finish line. The fans couldn't believe what they were seeing. All four racers crossed the finish line at the same moment, breaking the Rally Race record for the fastest time!

Lightning and the other racers drove up onto the winner's podium. They had all been awarded first place!

"What motivated all of you to race your best today?" asked a reporter.

"Well, we couldn't have done it without the *Waldgeister* monster," said Lightning.

Mater glanced back at the old gentlecar and gave him a wink.

Monsters, Inc.

What I Did on
My Summer Vacation

Mike sat in Boo's bedroom, telling jokes and acting silly. He was collecting laughs to help power the city of Monstropolis.

The little girl was happy to see the one-eyed monster, but she didn't laugh quite as much as usual.

"Is something wrong, Boo?" Mike asked.

Boo pointed to some hand-drawn pictures on her wall. There was one of her school, and another of kids holding up photos of places they had visited.

"School starts!" Boo said. "No photos!"

Mike quickly figured out what Boo meant. School was about to begin, and she was going to tell her class what she'd done over vacation—but she wanted a fun story, and she needed pictures.

"Why don't you come to Monsters, Inc., with me?" Mike suggested. "We'll surprise Sulley."

Boo and Mike went to Monsters, Inc., by stepping through Boo's closet
door.

"Follow me," said Mike. "I have something you can borrow." Mike knew
exactly how Boo could get photos for her class before she started school.

Mike took an old camera from the top of a supply closet. "Let's see if it still works," he said.

"*EEP!*" cried Mike at the flash.

Boo laughed so hard that the lights flickered. "Yup, I guess it works," he said.

Then Mike led Boo to the Laugh Floor.

"Oh, Sulleeey!" he called out to his furry blue friend. "I have a surprise for you."

"Kitty!" Boo exclaimed.

Sulley was so surprised to see Boo. He wrapped her in a big hug.

Sulley was happy to have his friend back with him again. It would be a great day!

Everyone on the Laugh Floor was excited to see Boo. Many of the monsters showed off their new tricks.

They had to work fast. Boo had school the next day! Mike knew they couldn't keep her out too late.

All night long, they raced from one place to another, all over Monsters, Inc.— and Monstropolis.

By the end of the visit, Boo had taken tons of photos. She and Mike were trying to decide which were the best ones to take to school.

Sulley frowned. "School? What do you mean 'school'?"

Mike explained Boo's hope for a great story and pictures to share with her class.

Sulley was not happy. "You know that's forbidden!" he exclaimed.

"Gee, Sulley, I was just trying to help," Mike said.

Sulley softened. "I know, Mikey, but it's my job to protect Monsters, Inc. We have to keep the monster world a secret from the human world."

"How are we going to tell Boo?" said Mike.

Sulley looked over his shoulder. Boo was already looking sad. Sulley hated to see Boo so disappointed.

"Please, Kitty?" she said.

Sully thought for a moment.

"Okay," Sulley said finally. "I'll let

you take back one photo. But I get to pick it."

Mike grinned, and Boo cheered.

At school the next day, Boo told her class all about her special adventure.

Her classmates didn't believe her. Her teacher didn't believe her.

So Boo pulled out the picture. . . .

The teacher gasped. "That looks like Bigfoot!"

Boo giggled. "Not Bigfoot. That's Kitty!"

A Winning Friendship

One sunny morning, Merida leapt out of bed and threw back the drapes. It was the perfect day for the DunBroch Games, a festival held in the spirit of fun and friendship.

Looking out the window, she saw clans arriving from across the kingdom. Merida could hardly wait to join the festivities—but first she had chores to do.

Walking out into the sunshine, Merida saw her parents, King Fergus and Queen Elinor. Standing between them was a boy.

"I want you to meet Kendrew," King Fergus said to Merida. "His father is a dear friend from a neighboring clan. I thought you could show him around."

Merida was thrilled. Now she could enjoy the games with someone her own age.

From the festival grounds, Merida heard the sound of cheering. "C'mon, Kendrew," she said. "The games are beginning!"

The cheers grew louder as the bagpipers and drummers signaled the start of the games.

Waving goodbye to her parents, Merida dragged Kendrew away.

Queen Elinor watched them go. "I hope they get along."

But King Fergus wasn't worried. "I'm sure it will be a winning friendship, my love. Now, which way was the caber toss?"

Merida knew where she wanted to go first—the archery field! Surely Kendrew would like to shoot a few arrows.

Kendrew nervously watched as Merida hit bull's-eye after bull's-eye. When it was his turn, Kendrew confessed, "I don't have a bow."

"Here," Merida said. "You can borrow mine."

Kendrew smiled at her kindness and reluctantly took the bow. But he wasn't the archer Merida was. In fact, he wasn't much of an archer at all. His arrows hit everything but the target. Every time he missed, his expression grew sadder.

"That's okay," Merida assured Kendrew. But she felt bad. She had just wanted to find something for them to do together. Then she had an idea. "What kind of events do you like?"

Instantly, Kendrew perked up. "C'mon, I'll show you!"

Kendrew led Merida toward a group of pipers. Scooping a set of bagpipes into his arms, he began playing.

Merida was confused. "But how do you win at bagpipes?" she asked.

"You don't," Kendrew replied. "You just play."

"Here, you try!" Kendrew said, and passed the instrument to Merida.

Holding bagpipes reminded Merida of wrestling her brothers on bath day.

And when she tried to play a tune . . . what a ruckus! Kendrew saw that Merida wasn't having any fun. Now *he* felt bad. "Let's go find something else to do," he suggested.

Merida and Kendrew continued to wander through the fairgrounds, but neither was having much fun. It seemed like whatever she liked, he didn't.

And whatever he enjoyed, she didn't.

Merida wondered if there was anything she and Kendrew could enjoy . . . together.

Just then, they came to the last tent at the festival. They stopped in front of a sign that read "Pet Costume Contest."

Kendrew sighed. "I've always wanted to enter the contest. I love to sew, but I don't have a pet to make a costume for."

Suddenly, Merida had an idea.

Merida told Kendrew
to wait for her
at the tent and
hurried off.
When she
returned,
Merida
wasn't alone.
She had brought
Angus!

"He's perfect!"
Kendrew exclaimed.

Merida was happy. Maybe this was
something they could do together.
They were both excited to make Angus
a new costume and win the contest!

Together they
set to work.

While Merida
schemed, Kendrew
sewed.

While
Kendrew cut,
Merida calmed.

While Merida
wiggled, Kendrew
wobbled.

Working as a team, they had created an outfit never
before seen (or worn) by man or beast.

When the contest ended, Merida and Kendrew had taken first prize!

"You were right, dear," said Queen Elinor, watching as the new friends rode off on Angus. "It was a winning friendship after all!"

Joe Gardner fought the urge to cover his ears. His middle school band students were playing a basic jazz number, but they couldn't keep up, keep time, or keep still.

That same day, Joe learned that his part-time teaching job had been made full-time. But Joe's dream was to *play* jazz. He believed it was what he was born to do—his true purpose.

Later that day, Joe's phone rang. It was Curley Baker, one of Joe's former students. He told Joe about an audition for the Dorothea Williams Quartet.

Joe hurried to the legendary jazz club The Half Note to audition with the quartet. When it was time for his solo, Joe closed his eyes, took a deep breath, and let the music flow. Afterward, Joe saw that everyone had stopped to listen. Dorothea Williams smiled and said, "Get a suit, Teach. A good suit. Back here tonight. First show's at nine. Sound check's at seven. We'll see how you do."

Joe walked through the city, chatting on his cell phone. "I got the gig!" Just then, Joe saw a motorcycle heading right for him. He stepped out of the way—and fell into an open manhole.

Joe's fall landed him on a moving sidewalk headed for a bright light in the distance. It was The Great Beyond! He turned and ran away from the light.

Joe ripped through a barrier and started falling again.

Then Joe landed in a beautiful bright meadow. A counselor named Jerry appeared and welcomed Joe to the You Seminar.

Jerry thought Joe was a lost mentor—a soul who had lived an amazing and inspiring life. Mentors helped new souls find their Spark and earn their Earth Pass.

Getting an Earth Pass would be Joe's ticket home!

Meanwhile, high above the moving sidewalk, the You Seminar's accountant, Terry, counted the souls as they passed. "There's a soul missing," she said. "The count's off."

The counselors assigned Joe a troublesome soul known as 22.

She had already been through hundreds of mentors, but Joe was unlike the others. He wanted to go back to Earth. The young soul couldn't believe it! She agreed to give him her Earth Pass as soon as they found her Spark.

The pair made their way to the Hall of Everything. But nothing inspired 22. She tried lots of professions, but still no Spark and no Earth Pass.

She took Joe to the Astral Plane and introduced him to a crew of quirky characters, the Mystics. They helped Joe open a portal to Earth. Joe closed his eyes, focusing on his body on Earth.

Joe could see himself lying in a hospital bed, a therapy cat curled in his lap. Joe was ready to jump through, but Moonwind was worried.

"N-n-no, Joe! Don't rush this! It's not the right time," the Mystic said.

Joe jumped anyway, accidentally knocking 22 into the portal with him.

A moment later, Joe cautiously opened his eyes. The good news was that he was in a body. The bad news? He was in the wrong body!

"No! No! No! No! No! NO! I'm in the cat? Wait a minute—if I'm in here, then who . . ." Joe looked at his body and realized 22 was in there.

She was horrified. "I'm in a body! Nooo!"

Joe did his best to stay calm. This was all Moonwind's fault, he decided.

"Okay," Joe said. "Gotta find Moonwind. He can fix this."

After escaping the hospital, Joe and 22 ended up on the streets of New York. The two soon found Moonwind spinning his sign at an intersection. The Mystic promised he would get Joe back into his body. "See you at The Half Note at six thirty. I'll take care of everything," Moonwind said.

Once they got to Joe's apartment, there was a knock on the door. It was Connie, from Joe's music class. She told Joe that she wanted to quit the trombone. But when Connie played, it was clear she loved music.

Inside Joe's body, 22 was feeling something she'd never felt before—*inspired*.

"I'll help you," 22 said, "but I . . . wanna try a few things while we're here. If Connie can find something she loves, maybe I can, too."

Later, an unexpected gust of wind knocked Joe's hat off. As 22 bent over to grab it, Joe's pants ripped at the seam! There was only one place where they could get the pants fixed in a hurry: Joe's mom's tailor shop.

For the first time, Joe was ready to tell his mom, Libba, exactly what his dream meant to him. He leaned in and told 22 just what to say.

"Look, if I'm doin' what I love, no matter how hard it is, I'll be fine."

Libba listened and smiled. Then she opened the closet and pulled out a surprise: Joe's dad's suit.

As Joe and 22 waited for Moonwind outside The Half Note, 22 watched a maple seed slowly spin to the ground. Maybe she hadn't found her Spark in the Hall of Everything because her Spark was walking, or sky watching. Joe didn't think those were real purposes. He told her she would have to keep trying to find her purpose when she got back to the You Seminar.

Upset, 22 ran down the street and ducked into the subway station. Joe was right behind her, meowing furiously. Then, out of nowhere, Terry appeared.

A portal scooped up Joe and 22, and their souls returned to the You Seminar.

Suddenly, the counselors were congratulating 22. She had earned her Earth Pass! But the young soul still had no idea what her Spark was.

She handed Joe her Earth Pass.

"It filled in because I was in your body, being *you*. It's your Spark that changed it, not mine," 22 said.

She slipped away, leaving Joe alone at the portal's edge. Joe was upset, but he needed to get back to Earth. Music was his purpose. It was what he was meant to do! Joe took the Earth Pass and jumped into the portal.

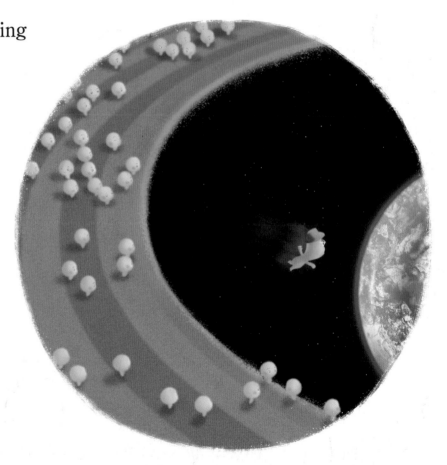

Back on Earth, Joe sat at The Half Note piano as the Dorothea Williams Quartet took the stage. He played perfectly, but later, after the show, Joe felt unfulfilled. He went home and played his piano. As he played more intently, he closed his eyes and entered the Zone. Then when he opened his eyes he was back in the Astral Plane.

Moonwind was waiting for Joe. Something was wrong . . . 22 wasn't herself. She had become a lost soul, angry and destructive. The enraged soul rampaged through the You Seminar. No one could stop her!

"No! Wait, 22! I was wrong!" Joe apologized, promising 22 she *was* ready for Earth. But 22 couldn't hear him. In a last desperate attempt, Joe reached out and placed a maple seed in 22's hand—a reminder of her love for Earth.

Joe gave 22 back her Earth Pass and walked her to the edge of the Earth Portal.

She and Joe leapt into the portal, and 22's Earth Pass began to glow. He smiled reassuringly as she let go of his hand and Joe returned, once more, to The Great Beyond.

Joe was back on the moving sidewalk when Counselor Jerry stopped him. Joe had inspired all the counselors, and they had a special gift for him. An Earth Portal materialized beside the sidewalk.

So Joe took one more fateful step, unsure of what lay ahead but prepared to appreciate each and every moment of his wonderful life.

Incredibles 2

A Day Out
with Mom

Helen beamed as she sat down to breakfast. Hero work had taken her away for quite a while, and she missed spending time with her family.

Helen knew Bob was still a little worn out from taking care of everything in her absence. "Why don't you go do something fun?" she suggested. "Take a little time for yourself and—"

Bob sprang up, kissed her on the cheek, and headed toward the door. "Thanks, honey!" he shouted. "See you all later!"

After breakfast, Helen had an idea. "Hey, Vi—"

"Yes, I'll watch Jack-Jack while you take Dash to track practice," Violet said.

"Actually, I was going to ask if you wanted to come with me," said Helen. "After we drop Dash off, I'll take you shopping for something to wear on your first date with Tony."

"I don't know," said Violet. "I was just going to wear something like . . . this." She gestured to her outfit.

"Come on," said Helen. "It'll be mother-daughter fun. You know, we can bond."

"Okay, Mom," Violet said with a chuckle.

171

Helen and the kids piled into the car and headed out.

They soon arrived at Dash's school and wondered why they were the only ones in the parking lot. "Oh, no," said Dash. "I forgot practice is canceled today!"

"Well . . . you can help with Jack-Jack," said Helen, upbeat. "Then Vi and I can focus on shopping."

"Great . . . babysitting," said Dash under his breath.

Helen and Violet began picking out things for Violet to try on, but Dash and Jack-Jack kept distracting them. When Jack-Jack spotted the mall carousel, he whined and shouted, "Babababa!" And Dash kept groaning as if he were in pain.

Helen handed Dash some cash. "Take your brother on the carousel and go enjoy the mall," she said, forcing a smile. "Meet us at the fountain in an hour."

"Thanks!" said Dash.

Jack-Jack clapped his hands, laughing and babbling as Dash wheeled him away.

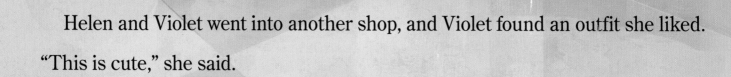

Helen and Violet went into another shop, and Violet found an outfit she liked.

"This is cute," she said.

"But so casual," said Helen. She held up a couple of dresses. "Look at these!"

Violet smiled and took them into the dressing room.

Meanwhile, Dash and Jack-Jack were having a blast. They rode the carousel and bought lots of candy. Then Dash counted their remaining money and grinned. Jack-Jack cackled as Dash pushed the stroller toward the train. The two jumped on.

"Now this is living," said Dash as he and Jack-Jack enjoyed their sweets in a train car.

At the end of the hour, Violet sat with Helen, feeling a little sad they hadn't found anything.

As Dash and Jack-Jack raced up to the fountain, Helen frowned.

"Sorry we're late," blurted Dash, showing off a colorful smile.

Before Helen could say a word, an alarm blared! A woman from the jewelry store shouted, "Thief!"

The family slapped on their masks and revealed their Supersuits. They darted into the jewelry store, but the thief was gone.

"He appeared out of nowhere," said the clerk. "He took the jewelry and vanished."

Elastigirl and the kids scanned the store, looking for clues.

Suddenly, another store alarm blared! The family took off toward it.

A chorus of alarms rang from every corner of the mall!

"Maybe it's a team of thieves," said Elastigirl.

"Or maybe he can multiply, like Jack-Jack," said Violet. Hearing that, Jack-Jack multiplied, and each baby wandered off in a different direction.

"I'll run around the mall and see if I can figure out what's going on," Dash said.

"We'll catch up with you," Elastigirl said.

Violet and Elastigirl collected as many Jack-Jacks as they could while Dash raced off to find the thief.

Dash spotted the burglar and could tell right away: he was definitely a

Supervillain. As Dash rushed toward him, he vanished in a flash of light.

Dash didn't notice the burglar reappear right behind him.

Elastigirl entered and stretched to try to grab the villain, but he disappeared and reappeared at a register behind her!

"Name's Blindspot," he said, disappearing again.

All the Jack-Jacks, Violet, Dash, and Elastigirl went after the thief.

Violet scooped up Jack-Jack and cued him to use his laser eyes. But Blindspot disappeared again! Even with Dash's super speed, he wasn't fast enough to catch the vanishing villain.

Elastigirl created a labyrinth of traps, hoping to trip him up. But Blindspot managed to disappear and reappear his way through the mall.

Then Violet caught Blindspot's reflection in a mirror and realized something: he was traveling through their blind spots! She quickly used a compact mirror to spot him, then threw a force field to trap him inside. The entire family ran alongside the Supervillain as he rolled through the mall.

Just then, a dress in a shop window caught Elastigirl's attention. "Vi! That'd look great on you!"

"Mom," said Violet, "I don't want to disappoint you, but . . . I don't really like dresses."

"I'm sorry, Vi," said Elastigirl. "I just wanted to spend some quality time with you."

Elastigirl anchored the force field to the fountain, locking the trapped Blindspot in place.

"Well, you got your wish," said Violet, smiling. "Nothing says family bonding like catching a Supervillain together!"

As the family headed out, Helen turned to Violet. "You know . . . I have no idea what I wore on my first date with your father. Clothes don't really matter. Wear something you like."

Later that week, Violet put on her favorite jeans and top and went downstairs.

"You look beautiful," said Helen.

"Thanks, Mom," said Violet, giving her mother a big hug. She was ready for her first date with Tony!

The Big Campout

"**G**uess what!" **Bonnie said** as she looked excitedly at all her toys. "We're going to do something really special tonight."

The toys were carefully arranged on Bonnie's bed. They couldn't wait to find out what the special something was! But they stayed motionless. The little girl clapped her hands with glee. "We're going on an adventure!" Bonnie cried.

The toys were excited, but they still didn't move.

"And we *all* get to go," Bonnie said. She carefully placed Woody, Buzz Lightyear, Slinky Dog, and all her new toys in a big tote bag. Next she collected her beloved old toys—Buttercup the unicorn, Trixie the triceratops, and a hedgehog called Mr. Pricklepants. A rag doll named Dolly came, too.

"We're going to have so much fun!" Bonnie told them.

Bonnie ran off to find a flashlight. Once she had left, all the toys suddenly came to life.

"I wonder where we're going," Mr. Pricklepants said.

"I hope there aren't any scary animals!" Rex the dinosaur whispered to his friends.

"I'll protect you," Woody said with a wink.

Then the toys heard footsteps and stopped talking.

"We're camping out!" Bonnie announced happily as she came back into the room. She scooped up the tote bag.

A few minutes later, Bonnie and her toys were in the backyard.

"Here we are!" she said. Bonnie carefully unpacked the toys and began arranging them inside a tent she had set up. "You sit next to Trixie," she told Rex, placing the two dinosaurs side by side. "Buttercup, Woody, and Buzz, you three will be next to my sleeping bag." Soon all the toys had their own spots.

"Now let's have a picnic!" Bonnie began passing out toy food and toy plates. "Corn for Buttercup, pepperoni pizza for Rex—"

"Bonnie! Dinnertime!" called Bonnie's mother.

Bonnie giggled. "I've got to go eat *my* dinner. But don't worry, I'll be back soon." She gave each toy a big hug, then crawled headfirst out of the tent.

Left alone in the tent, the toys began to explore.

"This is a right comfortable spot," Jessie said, admiring Bonnie's puffy sleeping bag.

"The accommodations really are quite satisfactory," Mr. Pricklepants agreed.

"Well, shine my spurs!" Woody exclaimed.

The cowboy walked over to an electric camping lantern. He turned it on, and a warm glow lit up the tent.

"Let's have a sing-along," Woody suggested. He held his cowboy hat over his heart and began to sing "Camptown Races."

Jessie quickly joined in, and Bullseye stomped his hooves in time to the beat. The other toys began singing, too.

After a few more songs, the toys went outside. They still had some time before Bonnie returned, and they wanted to explore.

Pushing through the tent flaps, the toys stepped into the backyard. It had grown dark.

"Look!" Buttercup said. "The stars are coming out!"

Buzz smiled. "That, my friend, is the Big Dipper—seven stars that form a ladle shape." He pointed toward the constellation.

"You sure know a lot about the sky," Trixie said, impressed.

Buzz grinned. "Comes with the space-ranger territory."

"I just saw a shooting star!" Mr. Potato Head shouted.

"I think that was a firefly," Hamm said.

Jessie hopped on Bullseye. "I'm going to explore the yard!"

Buttercup trotted over. "Follow me! I'll show you the rose bed."

Trixie turned to the other toys. "Who wants to play freeze tag?"

With a sly smile, she tapped Rex. "Tag. You're frozen!"

Smiling, the rest of the toys began running away as Trixie chased after them.

"The flower bed is out of bounds!" she shouted.

"Hey! Someone? Tag me?" Rex called, still frozen. "Anyone?"

"I'm wiped out," Hamm said a little while later.

"How about a shadow-puppet production?" Mr. Pricklepants suggested.

"That's a great idea," Woody said, leading his friends into the tent. "Bonnie's going to be back soon."

The toys used Bonnie's flashlight to create shadow puppets on the tent. Buzz made an airplane with his wings. Mr. Pricklepants made an elephant.

Rex peeked outside the tent window. "Boy, it sure got dark fast," he remarked.

Then Dolly made a pair of bunny ears behind the dinosaur's head. Everyone laughed, even Rex!

"A sleepover wouldn't be complete without a scary story," Mr. Potato Head said. He clicked off the flashlight. "Once there was a little toy that got lost in the forest. The forest was dark. Very dark."

"Just like now!" Rex exclaimed, beginning to get scared.

"Suddenly, there were footsteps," Mr. Potato Head said.

The toys heard the sound of someone running.

"Like now!" Jessie said with a gasp.

Mr. Potato Head continued his story. "A monster was coming—"

"Aaah!" Rex shrieked as a huge shadow loomed over the tent.

The toys all flopped down and went still.

The tent flap opened. . . .

It was Bonnie! She brought the toys outside and gave each one a marshmallow on a twig. "It wouldn't be a campout if we didn't toast marshmallows!" she announced happily.

The toys couldn't have agreed more. And Rex was especially glad that there wasn't a real monster after all!

Disney · PIXAR
INSIDE OUT

The Riley and Bing Bong Band

Riley and her imaginary friend, Bing Bong, loved making music

together.

The Riley and Bing Bong Band was Joy's favorite! But the

other Emotions weren't such big fans.

Anger thought the music was way too loud.

Fear kept a close eye on the instruments. Sadness

only liked the minor chords.

And just the sight of Bing Bong

playing his nose made Disgust

cringe.

One day, after

playing some new tunes,

Riley and Bing Bong took a break.

"We should go on tour!" said Riley.

"Great idea! Where should we go?" asked Bing Bong.

"How about Australia?" said Riley. "We can play for the kangaroos!"

"But how will we get there?" asked Bing Bong.

"We can take our rocket!" said Riley.

"Of course!" Bing Bong said. "The rocket!"

"Wooo-hooo!" exclaimed Joy. "A new adventure!"

"We'll get homesick," said Sadness.

Fear gathered information on Australia. "Koalas, wallabies, goannas! Look at those claws."

"Ugh! I can't . . . I just can't," said Disgust.

Anger brightened when he saw a picture of kangaroos boxing. "Do they really box? I'm liking this!"

"We're going to Australia," announced Riley to Mom and Dad.

"Be back for dinner," said Mom. "I'm making my famous mashed potatoes."

"Don't forget there's a big ocean between Minnesota and Australia," said Dad.

Riley whispered to Bing Bong. "We'd better bring our floaties."

Riley and Bing Bong packed up everything they needed and climbed into the rocket, preparing for liftoff.

Riley turned to Bing Bong. "Okay, copilot. Ready to check all systems?" They had to make sure their rocket was in tip-top shape for takeoff.

"Check," said Bing Bong pointing at the controls. "Check, check, and . . . check!"

"Activating rocket booster," said Riley. "Mission Control, all systems are go!"

Riley and Bing Bong began the countdown. "Ten, nine, eight, seven, six, five, four, three, two, one . . . *BLAST OFF*!"

But nothing happened.

Riley and Bing Bong were confused.

"Of course!" said Riley. "The rocket can't fly without fuel!"

Riley and Bing Bong smiled at each other and began to sing their special song.

"Who's your friend who likes to play?"

The rocket answered back, binging and bonging.

Then it rumbled and roared as it flew out the window!

As they soared over the ocean, Riley and Bing Bong saw a shark, a sea turtle, a walrus, and penguins. So far, this was the best trip ever.

Suddenly, Bing Bong
noticed the water
was getting closer.
"Are we landing?"
he asked.

Riley and Bing
Bong screamed as the
rocket fell toward
the big blue ocean!

Riley grabbed
the radio.
"Mission Control,
we have a problem!"

"It's over!" shouted Fear, hiding
his head inside a paper bag.

"I knew it," said Sadness.

"The fuel," said Joy. "We were so busy being excited, we forgot to sing!" She plugged in an idea bulb.

"We have to sing!" shouted Riley.

"I'm so scared! I can't remember the words!" said Bing Bong.

"Sing the song! *Sing the song!*" shouted Anger.

"Sing or we'll smell like seaweed!" yelled Disgust.

Riley shouted out the words as the rocket sputtered.

Bing Bong joined her, and the two sang louder and faster than ever before.

"Who's your friend who likes to play?

Bing Bong, Bing Bong!

His rocket makes you yell, 'Hooray!'

Bing Bong, Bing Bong!"

The rocket skimmed the surface of the ocean and then lifted back into the air! Riley and Bing Bong kept singing as the rocket soared.

Soon they could see land.

"Australia!" shouted Riley.

The Emotions cheered.

The creatures Down Under welcomed Riley and Bing Bong with big smiles.

"Play us a tune, mates," said a koala.

Riley and Bing Bong played all their songs, and the crowd went wild!

Suddenly, a familiar smell drifted through the air. "Mom's famous mashed potatoes," Riley whispered to Bing Bong. "It's time to go home."

They played one last song and then said goodbye to their new friends and rocketed back to Minnesota.

"It's nice to be home," said Sadness.

"Sure, it's nice to be home, but traveling is so cool!" said Joy.

"I beg to differ," said Fear. "I like staying right here in good ol' Minnesota. No more trips for this guy."

"So . . . how was Australia?" asked Dad.

"It was great!" said Riley. "Tomorrow we're going on another trip— to play for the penguins in Antarctica."

"Yes!" Joy shouted. "Noooooooooooo!" Fear screamed before he fainted onto the floor.

You're It, Dory!

After school, **Nemo, Marlin,** Dory, and all their friends decided to play a game of hide-and-seek. Dory was it first! Everyone swam to find a hiding place as she began to count. "One . . . two . . . three . . . um . . . four . . . um . . . um . . ." Dory said.

When Dory opened her eyes, she forgot why she was counting!

"Hmmm, what was I about to do? Lie and sneak? No. Why would I do that? Spy and peek? No . . . that can't be right. Oh! Hide-and-seek!" she said, swimming off toward Nemo and Marlin's anemone, hoping to find them there.

Dory sang to herself as she swam toward her friends' home. She was excited for a game!

But by the time Dory got to their anemone, she'd forgotten why she went. She kept swimming closer. She had a nagging feeling she shouldn't get too close, but she couldn't remember why. . . .

"YEEOWCH!" she exclaimed. "Now I remember. I'm not supposed to touch anemones because they sting!"

As she swam away, rubbing her stung fin, Marlin and Nemo peeked out from their anemone.

"Where's she going, Dad?" Nemo asked. "She was so close to finding us!"

"I'm not sure . . ." Marlin responded.

"Hmm, what was I doing again?" Dory asked herself. She tried her best to remember, but she kept getting distracted and swimming right past all her friends.

"My spot is so good!" Pearl whispered to Bob after Dory swam by.

"Mine too! I love hide-and-seek," Bob whispered back.

"Wait! Wasn't I playing hide-and-seek?" Dory said, finally remembering.

"Wow, that guy looks a lot like Hank," Dory said.

"What color is he again? Yellow? No. Pink? Nope, I don't think so. Blue?"

Dory continued to swim through the coral field, and Hank tried his best to blend in with his surroundings as she got closer to him.

"That was a close call," Hank said to himself when Dory eventually swam away to seek another friend.

But as Dory swam through the Great Barrier Reef, she forgot again she was playing hide-and-seek.

She swam right past Bailey, who was hiding behind some seaweed, and even swam right *over* Destiny, who was hiding on the ocean floor.

Dory was having a very nice day. She had explored her little part of the ocean. She had seen pretty coral in the coral field and everything the Great Barrier Reef had to offer.

As Dory kept swimming, she spotted a beautiful purple shell on the sand.

"My mom loves shells!" she said. "I should give this one to her. But I haven't seen my mom or dad in a while. Actually, I haven't seen any of my friends. Where are they?"

That's when Dory remembered they were playing a game of hide-and-seek . . . but not that she was it!

"Uh-oh, I better find a hiding spot quick!" she said.

Dory's parents, Charlie and Jenny, watched from their hiding place as Dory swam into a nearby cave. They expected her to come out once she realized no one was hiding there, but after a couple of minutes they started to worry.

They agreed that they should go check on their daughter. Shortly after entering the cave, they found Dory.

"Kelpcake, what are you up to?" Charlie said.

"Mom! Dad! We're playing hide-and-seek, and I found this *great* hiding spot! Come in, I'll make room," Dory told them.

"But, sweetie—" Jenny tried to explain that everyone was hiding from Dory, but before she could, Dory swam to the opening of the cave.

Dory saw Hank and Mr. Ray swimming past the cave and wanted to help them hide, too. "Okay, okay, everybody in. We can squeeze," she told them.

"But, Dory—" Mr. Ray began, but before he could get another word out, Dory saw even more of her friends in need of a hiding spot. Nearly everyone who was supposed to be hiding from Dory was in the cave with her! "It's gonna be tight," she said to her friends.

Dory had almost all her friends in the cave with her.

This is so nice, Dory thought. *All my friends in one place . . . except . . .* Dory realized she was missing Nemo and Marlin. She wondered what they were doing. And then she quickly forgot what she had been wondering.

Finally, Nemo and Marlin wandered into the cave. They were shocked to find all their friends crowded in with Dory!

"Dory," Nemo said, "what are you doing?"

"Nemo! We are . . . hmmm . . . What *are* we doing?"

"Playing hide-and-seek!" everyone shouted.

The group swam out of the cave as Nemo explained what had happened.

"But you're it, Dory. You're supposed to be looking for *us*."

"Oh. I see. . . . Found you!" Dory exclaimed.

Marlin had a solution. "Let's just play tag."

A Delicious Duo

Alfredo Linguini walked into his restaurant one morning to the smell of a delicious mushroom-and-cheese omelet. He entered the kitchen to find his friend Remy cooking up a wonderful breakfast for the two of them.

"What a great surprise. This looks really good!" Linguini said.

As they ate, Remy noticed his friend was quieter than usual.

"This surprise reminded me that today is Colette's birthday," Linguini said with a sigh. "And I have no idea what to get her. Maybe some flowers? Or, ah . . . a hat, or—"

Remy thought they could make Colette a nice meal for her birthday, so he picked up his favorite cookbook.

"Hey," Linguini said, seeing the book. "This gives me an idea. I can *cook* her something! I bet she'd love that!"

Remy sighed with relief, glad Linguini had figured out the same perfect birthday plan.

Linguini landed on a recipe he thought even
he could cook: *scoglio*, a seafood pasta.

Remy nodded and began running around
the kitchen collecting the ingredients they'd
need. Whatever he didn't find, Linguini
wrote on a list to take to the supermarket.

Linguini also added a note to get flowers.
Remy thought that idea was pretty good, too.

Once Linguini had the final list, he headed for the door. "Thanks for your help, Little Chef."

Remy jumped up on his ladder, ready to join Linguini.

"I really appreciate all your help," Linguini said, "but since this is a special gift from me to Colette, I think I, uh, I want to do this on my own."

But when he got to the supermarket, he saw there were ten ingredients needed . . . just for the pasta sauce! Linguini headed down the closest aisle and saw premade jars of pasta sauce. He knew Remy would never approve, but with so little time, he decided to grab a sauce and move on.

Next on the list were some vegetables. The cookbook instructions had listed detailed steps for chopping and dicing and spiralizing, so he was happy to find a freezer full of precut veggies.

After the supermarket, Linguini headed for the fish market and flower stand by the river.

The list said to buy fresh fish, like mussels, scallops, or shrimp. But Linguini spotted a sign advertising live lobsters. *That's as fresh as fish can get!* Linguini thought. He bought the largest lobster at the fish market, quickly grabbed a bouquet of flowers, and was on his way!

When Linguini returned to the restaurant, Remy was shocked to see that he'd hardly followed the list at all!

But Remy knew that a good chef could make a great meal out of any ingredients, so he hopped up on the counter and began to revise the dinner plan.

"Whoa, what are you doing?" Linguini asked. "I've got it from here. Why don't you sit down and, uh, relax?"

Half an hour into cooking, Linguini was a little surprised everything was going so smoothly—until he turned around to see Remy testing the sauce.

"Little Chef!" Linguini exclaimed. "I know you're just trying to help, but

I really want to do this by myself. You know? I just want to try."

Remy understood. Linguini was trying to do something from the heart,

and Remy wanted to let his friend do just that.

With Remy gone, Linguini tried his best to pay extra-close attention to what he was doing . . . but things quickly fell apart.

Just when Linguini thought the situation couldn't get any worse, the sauce exploded all over the kitchen!

Linguini sank to the floor and called for his friend. "Little Chef!"

Remy ran into the kitchen and sat down next to Linguini.

"I'm sorry, pal," Linguini said. "I wanted this gift to be from me to her, but I think we'll create something even more special together. Would you help me finish cooking? Colette deserves a great meal on her birthday, and I know with your help I can make one."

Remy got up and began running around the kitchen. Then he started flipping through the cookbook, searching for a different recipe.

Eventually, Remy found something they could make together using what Linguini had left from the store and what Remy had in the restaurant.

Remy hopped on Linguini's head to get to work.

Just as they finished cooking, Colette arrived.

Linguini led her to a table. "Linguini by Linguini . . . and Little Chef!" he announced.

"This food smells amazing!" she exclaimed, smiling. "How'd you know this was my favorite pasta? And flowers, too!"

Linguini and Remy shared a knowing look.

"I had a bit of help." Linguini chuckled. "Happy birthday, Colette."

A New Purpose

Lightning flashed across the sky as Andy ran into his room with an armful of toys, but he had accidentally left RC outside. When Andy went downstairs, Woody headed to Andy's sister's room to search for the lost toy.

Bo and Woody came up with a plan. Slinky Dog stretched his springy body out the window as Woody scrambled down his back to rescue RC.

Moments later, though, Andy's mom came to get Bo and her sheep. Andy's sister, Molly, was giving them away!

Woody snuck over to Bo as she stood in the cardboard box. He wanted to help her escape and take her back to Andy's room, but Bo was ready to go.

Years passed, and eventually a much older Andy gave his toys to a little girl named Bonnie. She loved them as much as Andy had, but things were different for Woody. He wasn't the favorite toy anymore.

When Bonnie was ready for her first day of kindergarten, Woody still decided to go with her . . . just in case she needed him.

She got upset at craft time, but he came to her rescue and brought her more art supplies when her head was turned. Bonnie used her imagination to put them together to make a new friend . . . Forky! By the end of the day, Bonnie loved Forky so much she decided to take him home.

To Woody's surprise, Forky came to life, just like the other toys.

Back in Bonnie's room, Woody introduced Forky to Bonnie's other toys.

"Bonnie made a new friend in class," he told them. "She literally *made* a new friend. Everyone, I want you to meet Forky!"

But wide-eyed Forky was *not* interested in being a toy.

"He was made from trash," Woody explained. "I know this is a little strange, but Forky is *the* most important toy to Bonnie right now."

The next morning, Bonnie and her family were going on a road trip. She loaded up the RV with her toys, including her new favorite, Forky.

One evening, Buzz Lightyear broke the news to Woody that Forky was climbing out of the moving RV. The plastic utensil jumped out the window! Woody knew he had to follow. He couldn't leave a toy behind!

Woody found Forky, and they walked to the next town to reunite with the RV. But something in the window of an antique store caught Woody's eye— Bo's lamp!

Woody and Forky entered the store, but instead of Bo, they found a doll named Gabby Gabby. Woody introduced himself and Forky, but Gabby Gabby wasn't all that interested in Forky.

Instead, she pointed at the voice box sewn into Woody's chest. "You have what I need. Right inside there," she said.

Woody escaped to the playground—but without Forky.

Before he could come up with a plan, a busload of campers overran the playground. In the middle of the mayhem, Woody spotted Bo Peep and her sheep. She was part of a group of toys that traveled around to find kids to play with.

The two friends couldn't have been happier to see each other! Bo even agreed to help rescue Forky.

Meanwhile, Buzz Lightyear had decided to search for Woody and Forky. The brave space ranger followed their trail through a carnival, but he was captured and placed on a prize wall. He met some new toys, Ducky and Bunny, who helped him escape.

Buzz found Woody and Bo, and the whole group snuck into the store to rescue Forky.

Bo pointed to a glass cabinet across the way. "That's most likely where your Forky is being kept."

Getting to it meant crossing a wide aisle that was patrolled by Dragon, the shop's tough-looking cat!

Woody wanted to get Forky *fast*! He ran across the aisle and climbed up to the cabinet, but it was locked.

Gabby Gabby's dummies surrounded the toys and captured Bo's sheep. The toys escaped, but Gabby Gabby had Forky *and* the sheep.

Bo needed to come up with a new plan. She took Woody to meet Duke Caboom—Canada's greatest stuntman. Bo thought Duke could jump across the aisle to the cabinet and rescue Forky and her sheep.

But Duke wanted no part of it. He remembered how he'd disappointed his kid when he failed to make a big jump. That was long before, and Duke hadn't jumped since.

"Be the Duke you are right now," Bo encouraged, "the one who jumps and crashes."

But Duke didn't make it! He crashed right into Dragon.

Woody urged everyone to try again to help him rescue Forky. But the toys were banged up and hurt.

Bo was upset that Woody was being so single-minded, so she led her lost toys back to the carnival.

Woody went back into the store alone to find Forky but instead came face to face with Gabby Gabby.

Woody listened as she explained how her voice box had never worked properly, so she'd never been any kid's favorite toy.

Woody understood how she felt. He decided to give her his voice box in exchange for Forky.

Woody knew he'd need Bo's help to find a kid for Gabby Gabby, and luckily, Bo agreed.

While Woody encouraged Gabby Gabby to be who she really was, Bo helped find the perfect little girl for her. She found someone who was lost and needed a friend. It was a perfect match! Gabby Gabby finally had a kid to love.

Woody and the other toys made their way back to Bonnie's RV. Everyone was happy to see Woody, and he was even happier to see Bonnie reunited with Forky. He had done the job he'd set out to do.

It was then he realized that there were kids and toys everywhere who would need his help.

Woody knew that wherever he went and whichever toy he helped next,

he'd always have his friends by his side.

They were partners now—to infinity and beyond.

THE GOOD DINOSAUR

Arlo's Birthday Adventure

Arlo was so excited! The next day was the triplets' seventh birthday, and every year Momma and Poppa planned a special day away from the farm.

"Well, Momma," Poppa said when he came back in from the field, "would you look at these young'uns? Why, they look like they're just about old enough for an adventure!"

Buck and Libby were excited. Arlo gulped. An adventure? That sounded scary. Surely his parents wouldn't plan anything too scary. Would they?

Momma smiled. "We're going for a picnic by my favorite waterfall. It's where Poppa and I met, you know."

"Seeing the waterfall is only part of the fun," Poppa said. "First we have to get there. And, boy, climbing to a waterfall can be quite an adventure!"

The next morning they set off bright and early.

Buck and Libby groaned. They hated getting up before sunrise. But Arlo had barely slept. All night he'd been worrying about the hike. What if he got lost? What if he stepped on something and got hurt? There was a lot that could go wrong on a hike.

Arlo looked over at Momma and started to smile. She was carrying a basket of his favorite berries. Maybe the hike wouldn't be so bad after all.

It wasn't long before Arlo's belly started to grumble. "Momma, I'm hungry," he said. "Can I have some berries?"

But Momma just shook her head. "The berries are for your birthday picnic, Arlo. Come along. There will be plenty to eat when we get to the waterfall!"

Arlo sighed and kept walking. It was his birthday. Why should he have
to wait?

Suddenly, Arlo stopped in his tracks. He'd been so busy thinking about
eating that he hadn't noticed when everything around him got darker.
Without realizing it, he'd followed Momma right into a dark forest!

Up ahead, Momma, Poppa, Buck, and Libby happily continued on their way. They hadn't even noticed that Arlo wasn't with them anymore.

Arlo's eyes darted back and forth as he followed the path. Strange shadows lurked in the trees, and sharp branches poked him as he ran.

"Momma!" he shouted. "Wait up!"

Momma turned around and slowed down, letting Arlo catch up to her. Arlo ran as fast as his little legs could take him. He didn't want to be caught out in the woods without his family.

By the time Arlo caught up with the rest of his family, they were climbing a very muddy hill. Arlo looked ahead at his siblings, already in the mud, and thought he'd had enough adventuring for the day. "Momma," he called. "Can I have some berries now?"

But Momma shook her head again. "Not until we get to the waterfall," she said. "Come on, Arlo. We're almost there, but be careful. The mud is slippery."

Arlo started to climb. He hadn't taken more than three steps when something slid past him. It was Buck!

"Yahoo!" Buck shouted, sliding through the mud on his back. "This is awesome!"

At the top of the hill, Arlo could see Libby running around the trees and jumping out at Momma and Poppa. "Boo!" she shouted, making Poppa laugh.

Slowly but steadily, Arlo continued up the muddy hill.

"Come on, slowpoke," Buck called, running past him. "Last one to the waterfall doesn't get any berries!"

Arlo put his head down and continued climbing. "I can do this. At least I think I *maybe* can." He climbed a bit farther and stumbled on a rock along the way. "It's my birthday. I can do *anything* today. And I'm *not* going to let Buck eat my birthday berries!"

Finally, Arlo reached the top of the hill. He found his family staring at a giant fallen tree.

"What's wrong?" he asked.

Momma pointed at the tree. "This is the path we usually take to the waterfall, but it's blocked. We'll have to go another way."

Poppa looked around. "It looks like our only choice is across these fallen rocks. That cave there might be a dead end," he said. "Whaddaya think, Momma?"

Momma nodded. "I think you're all big enough now to handle a few fallen rocks. And besides, look at the waterfall right on the other side of them! That's the one."

Poppa set off across the rocks, with Libby and Buck close behind him. Arlo went next. He slowly stepped over one rock, then another. He was going to reach that waterfall if it was the last thing he did!

But as Momma started up the path, she tripped. The basket of berries went flying, and the berries rolled into the nearby cave.

"No!" Arlo shouted. He'd gone all that way, and he was *not* going to miss eating his birthday berries. He turned around and ran straight into the dark cave.

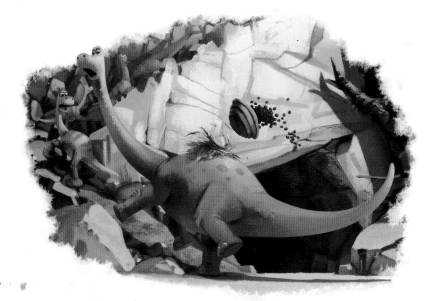

"What happened to Arlo?" Libby asked.

"He just turned around and ran into that cave," Momma explained.

Buck looked at the dark cave. "Arlo went in there? No way."

Arlo emerged from the cave. In his mouth was the basket, and it was full of berries! He gently set it down.

"Hey, guess what!" Arlo called out. "The cave isn't a dead end. And it leads right to the waterfall!"

"I can't believe you went in there alone," Buck said.

"Weren't you scared?" Libby added.

Arlo gestured to the basket. "Well, Momma picked these berries and carried them all this way. Now, come on! We've got a waterfall to see."

Arlo picked up the basket again and turned around to walk back through the tunnel. His family followed.

Poppa smiled at Momma. "It looks like our boy is growing up."

"That he is," Momma said, taking the berries from Arlo and setting them beside the waterfall. "Now, I think it's time for that birthday picnic. And the first berries go to Arlo, for saving the day!"

"Aaah," Arlo said as he happily munched on his berries and looked at the waterfall. "I guess some things are worth waiting for, after all."

Luca

A Gift for Giulia

Luca, Alberto, and Giulia were best friends. They did everything together. They ate together. They played together. They even won the Portorosso Cup together! Not only were they friends, but they were a team. And teammates stick together.

"Underdogs forever!"

They had so much fun during the summer, going on adventure after adventure. They loved to ride around town on their Vespa together and just enjoy being kids. But they knew summer couldn't last forever.

The days were getting shorter. The weather would soon be cooling down. All over Italy, schools were opening their doors. Summer was ending, and Giulia was leaving.

Luca watched as she packed her suitcase. It was going to be months before he saw her again.

"I'm sure gonna miss you guys. Here," she said, grabbing a stack of old schoolbooks that she knew Luca liked. "Every time you read these books, you'll think of me."

"Thanks, Giulia!" said Luca. Then he realized something.

"We need to get Giulia a gift," he whispered to Alberto. "So she can remember us, too."

"Yes!" said Alberto. "But not just any old gift. We'll get her something so awesome, she'll remember us forever!" He scratched his chin. "But what? Something from underwater?"

"Underwater?" asked Giulia, stepping between them. "Santa Pecorino! That's a great idea!"

The next morning, Giulia met the boys at the beach. It was an exciting day! She had never been to Luca's home before. As Giulia got into her diving suit, Alberto jumped into the water . . .

. . . and transformed into a sea monster!

Luca and Giulia joined Alberto underwater. They began swimming down toward the ocean floor.

"You guys live all the way down here?" Giulia asked.

"Yeah," said Alberto with a shrug. "We're pretty cool."

"I can't wait to show you around," said Luca.

"This way!" said Alberto.

They arrived in a seagrass meadow.

"It's beautiful!" said Giulia. "What is this place?"

"This is where I help out on the family goatfish farm," said Luca. *WHOOSH!*

A school of goatfish appeared, swimming this way and that, colliding and bumping into one another.

Luca swam all around trying to direct them, but no matter how hard he tried, the fish still swam out of order.

"Can I try?" Giulia asked.

"Hey, boys!" called Giulia a few minutes later. "Check it out!"

Luca's mouth dropped open. The goatfish were swimming in a perfect figure eight. Not a single fish was out of place! Even Alberto was impressed.

"How did you do that?" Luca asked.

Giulia beamed. "I got them to work as a team. And teammates stick together!"

Next they went to Luca's house.

"Here, have a coral cookie. You can eat it when you get

back to the surface," said Luca's mom.

Then Luca's dad showed Giulia his prize show crabs.

"This is Pinchy-pessa, the fastest and feistiest crab in the seven seas."

"She's amazing," said Giulia. "I wish my dad could see this."

Luca's dad had an idea. He gave Giulia a crab of her own!

Luca couldn't believe it. Even his parents had figured out the perfect gifts for Giulia! He searched his bedroom but didn't find anything that would be a good gift.

"Looking for something?" his grandma asked.

"Yeah," he said. "A gift for Giulia. Do you have any ideas?"

"It's Saturday," she reminded him. "Let's try the farmers market."

Every week, everyone in Luca's village gathered on a large sandbar to sell their merchandise. Giulia was so enthralled by all the colors and sounds that she forgot to say even one "Santa Pecorino."

The local sea monsters were just as distracted by Giulia. They had never seen a land monster underwater!

Luca and Alberto searched the stalls for an amazing gift idea, hoping something would catch their eye.

They tried a stall that displayed beautiful pearls in many different colors.

Luca picked out a small one. It was red like Giulia's hair.

"This is perfect!" he said. "How much?"

When the farmer told him, he quickly put the pearl back.

"What do we do now?" asked Luca.

"I'll tell you what we do!" said Giulia, swimming up behind them. "Join the crab race! C'mon!"

The contestants placed their crabs at the starting line. Giulia cheered for her crab alongside Luca's grandma and parents.

"You got this!" she yelled.

The crabs scuttled as fast as they could, but they were no match for Giulia's. It went so fast, it passed the others—twice!

The crowd cheered as it crossed the finish line. First place!

"Woo-hoo!" cheered Giulia. She had a huge grin on her face, and her crab wore a first-place sea star on its shell. But she noticed Luca was looking sad.

"Hey, what's the matter?" she asked.

Luca sighed. "We wanted to get you a gift," he confessed. "Something for you to remember us by. But we haven't been able to find anything good."

"Santa Gorgonzola! Are you kidding?" Giulia said. "This day has been the best gift ever. I'll remember this forever!"

She wrapped them in a big hug.

"I'm going to miss you guys. You'll have to tell me all about your adventures when I get back."

Alberto snapped his fingers.

"That's it!" he said. "I'm about to be awesome. Follow me!"

They followed him back to his hideout. Inside were all the human things Alberto had collected over the years.

"Here it is. A writey-thingy!" he said proudly.

Giulia scratched her head. "You mean a pen? But I've already got school supplies."

"This isn't for school," said Alberto. "This is for drawing awesome flames! And making secret maps! And"—he handed the pen to Giulia—"for writing us letters while you're away."

Luca beamed. So did Giulia.

"That *is* a good gift," Luca said.

The three friends sat together on the roof and looked out toward
Portorosso. Luca and Alberto had found the perfect gift for Giulia. But
being together in that moment? That was the most perfect gift of all!